Farrar Straus Giroux Books for Young Readers
An imprint of Macmillan Publishing Group, LLC
175 Fifth Avenue, New York, NY 10010

Color separations by Embassy Graphics
Printed in China by Shaoguan Fortune Creative Industries Co. Ltd.,
Shaoguan, Guangdong Province
Designed by Roberta Pressel
First edition, 2018
10 9 8 7 6 5 4 3 2 1

ISBN: 978-0-374-30447-8

poutpoutfish.com

The Pout-Pout Fish Look-and-Find Book

Deborah Diesen

Pictures by Dan Hanna

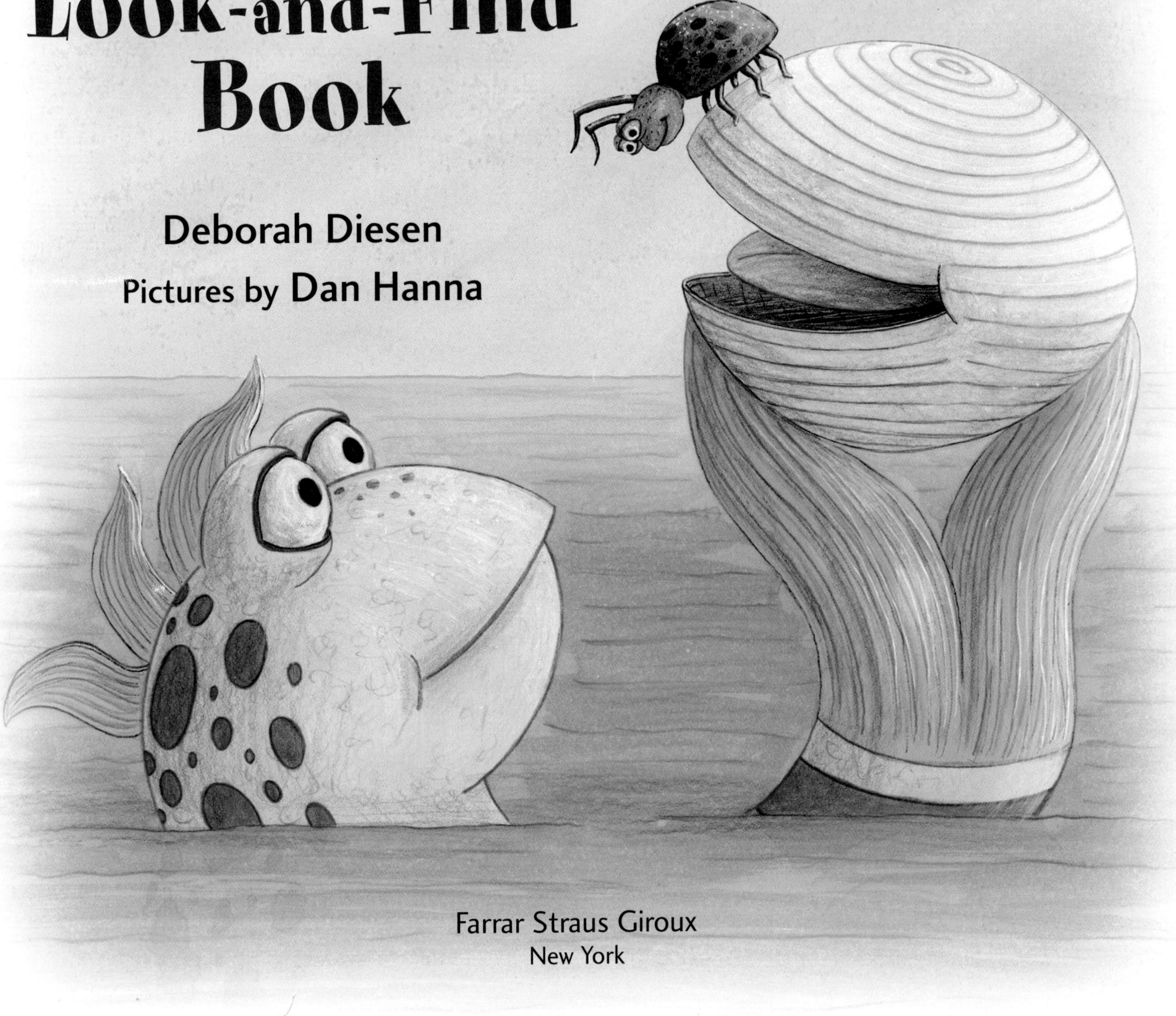

Farrar Straus Giroux

New York

POUT-POUT FISH IS LOOKING FOR SEA CREATURES.
FIND THESE OBJECTS HIDDEN IN THE BIG PICTURE.

POUT-POUT FISH IS UPSIDE-DOWN!
HE NEEDS YOUR HELP TO FIND THESE
OBJECTS HIDDEN IN THE BIG PICTURE.

PEANUT
BUTTER

THERE ARE SO MANY COLORFUL PLANTS AROUND THE TINYTANIC SHIPWRECK! FIND THESE OBJECTS HIDDEN IN THE BIG PICTURE.

TInyTANIC

WHAT IS POUT-POUT FISH LOOKING FOR? FIND THESE OBJECTS HIDDEN IN THE BIG PICTURE.

BE VERY QUIET! MOST OF THESE FISH ARE FAST ASLEEP.
FIND THESE OBJECTS HIDDEN IN THE BIG PICTURE.

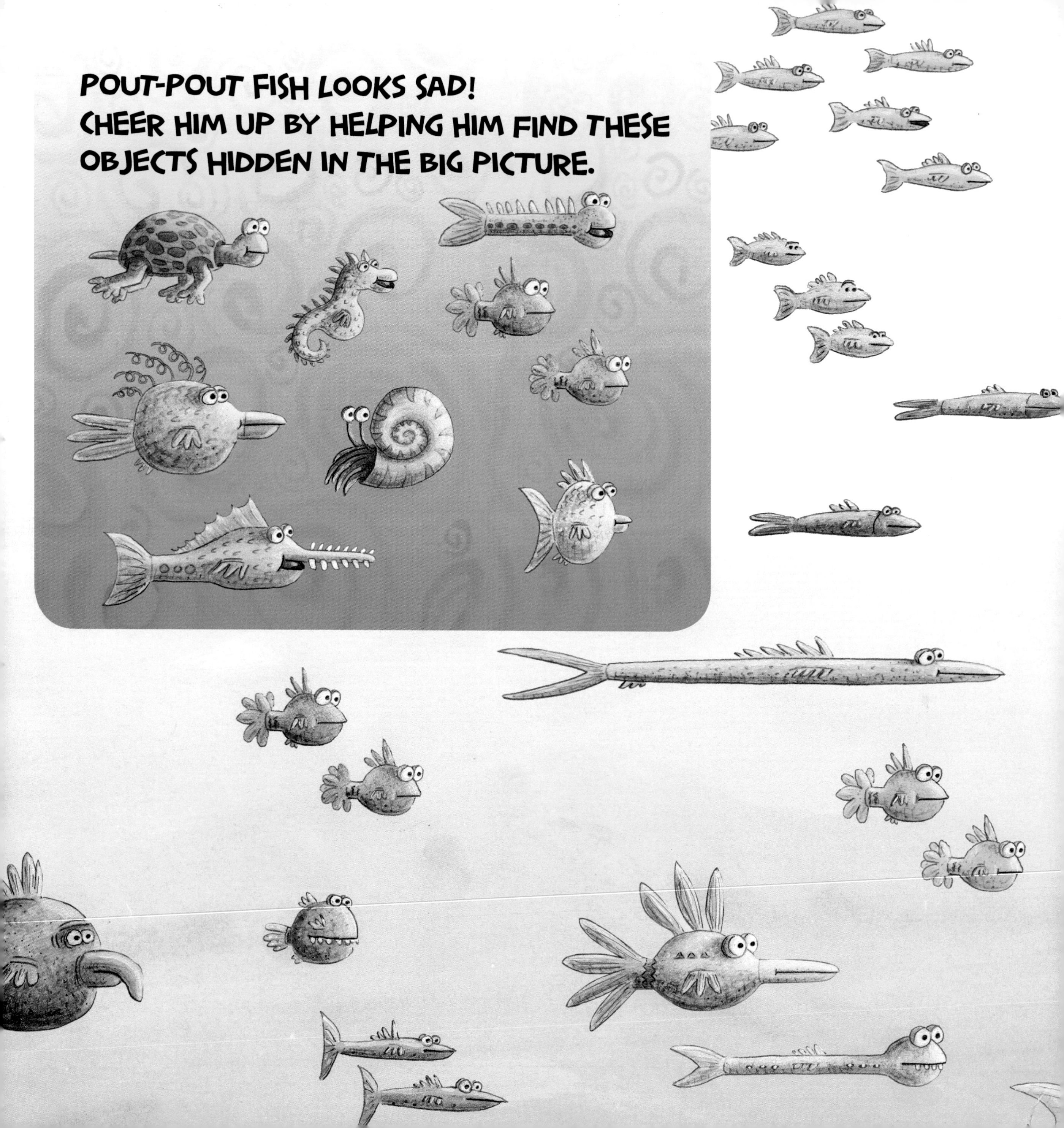
POUT-POUT FISH LOOKS SAD!
CHEER HIM UP BY HELPING HIM FIND THESE OBJECTS HIDDEN IN THE BIG PICTURE.

MISS SHIMMER WANTS TO GIVE POUT-POUT FISH A SMOOCH! FIND THESE OBJECTS HIDDEN IN THE BIG PICTURE.

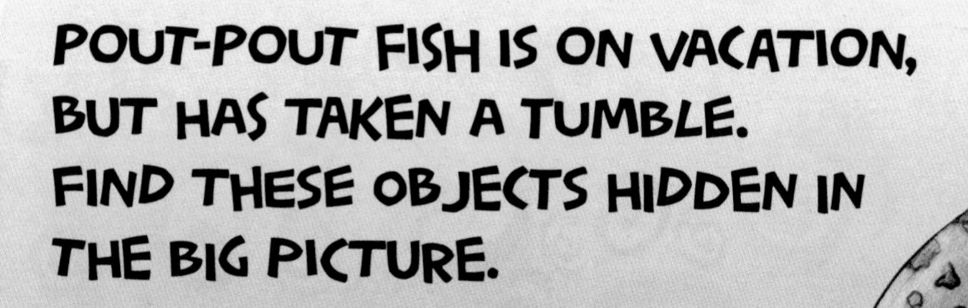

POUT-POUT FISH IS ON VACATION, BUT HAS TAKEN A TUMBLE. FIND THESE OBJECTS HIDDEN IN THE BIG PICTURE.

POUT-POUT FISH IS HOME!
FIND THESE OBJECTS HIDDEN IN THE BIG PICTURE.

MR. FISH

WELCOME HOME
MR.
FISH

POUT-POUT FISH AND MISS SHIMMER ARE MAKING GIFTS FOR THEIR FRIENDS.
FIND THESE OBJECTS HIDDEN IN THE BIG PICTURE.

IT'S HOLIDAY TIME!
FIND THESE OBJECTS HIDDEN IN THE BIG PICTURE.

FRIENDS MAKE THE WORLD GO 'ROUND! FIND THESE OBJECTS HIDDEN IN THE BIG PICTURE.